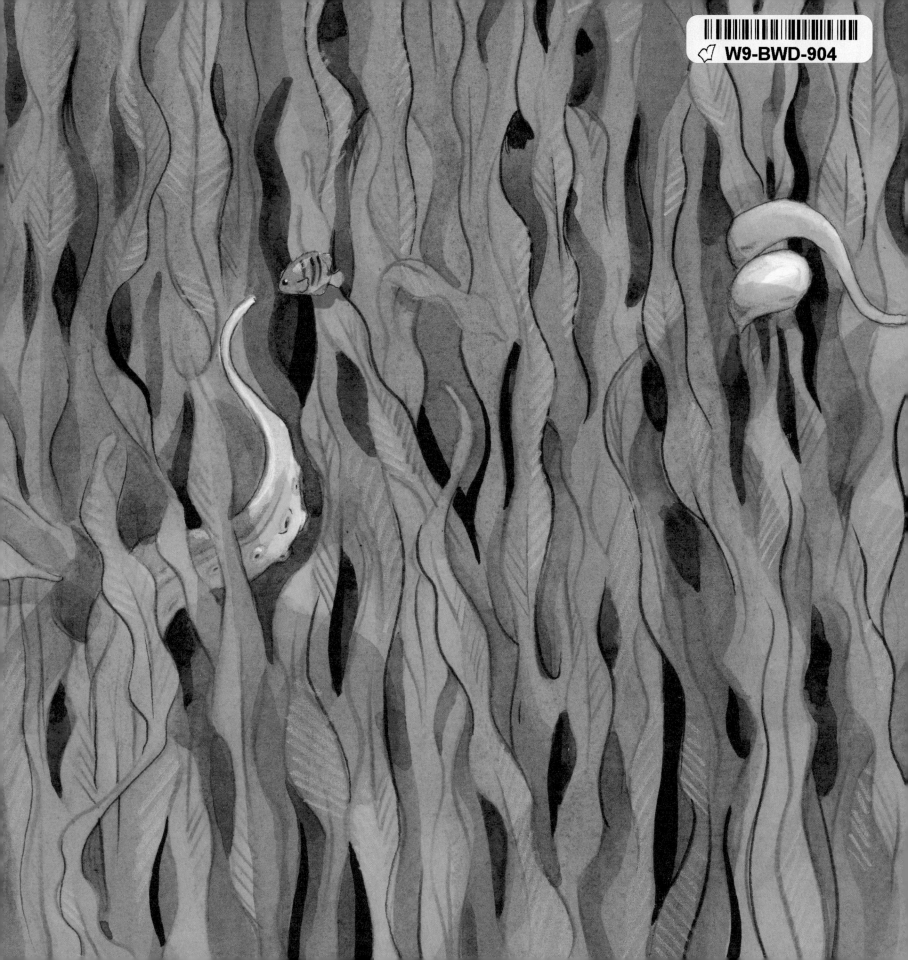

Inky THE OCTOPUS

words by **Erin Guendelsberger**

art by **David Leonard**

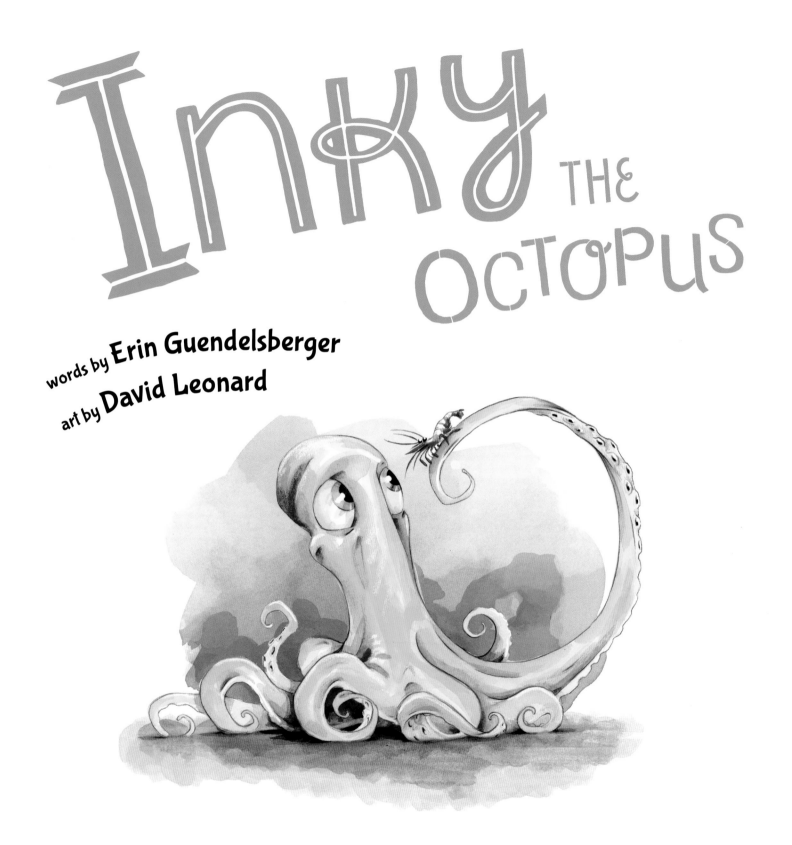

sourcebooks
jabberwocky

I live in a world of see-through walls,
in a tank with a locked-down lid.
I'm fed like a king three meals a day
of lobster, shrimp, and squid.

I know I have a good life
and should want for nothing more.
But something tugs at my curious heart
that I simply can't ignore.

Out of this tank, I must be free.
I must explore the open sea!

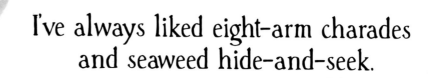

I've always liked eight-arm charades
and seaweed hide-and-seek.

I've had fun playing gravel hockey
and tentacle tag each week.

But I long to see a brand new world
of plants and rocks and fish.
Discovering things I've never known
has become my only wish.

Out of this tank, I must break free.
I hear the ocean calling me!

What is this? Tonight, it seems,
  my tank lid is ajar.
This could be my one chance for change—

dare I hope that far?

I tell my tank mate Blotchy
    we should bid our tank "Adieu."
I tell him we'll be happier,
    exploring someplace new.

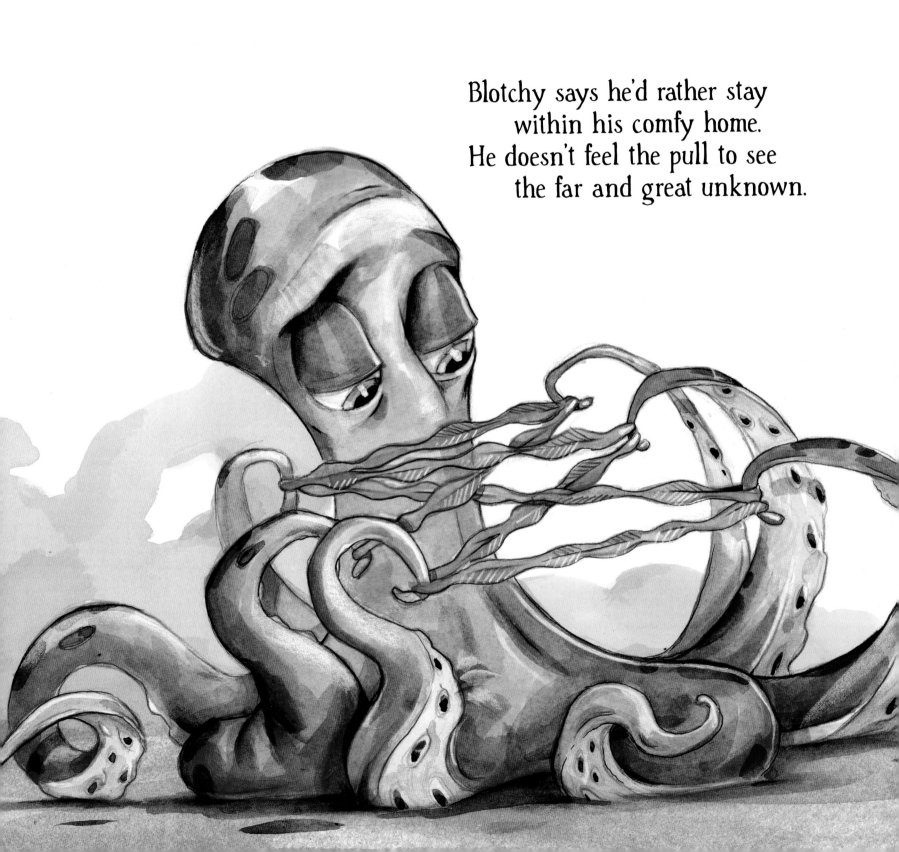

Blotchy says he'd rather stay
within his comfy home.
He doesn't feel the pull to see
the far and great unknown.

And so this quest I must take on
is one I'll take alone.

I'll be a solo traveler
when I set off to roam.

Out of this tank, I must break free.
My heart flies to the open sea!

Here I go, to the top of the tank!
    I slide one arm outside.
The air in the room feels dry and cool.
    The space feels free and wide.

I lift through arms two, three, and four!
Next five, six, seven, eight!

My head is last, and then I'm sliding
down the tank's glass plate.

The floor feels strange beneath me.
Odd noises fill the room.

The air smells different from my tank:
it's freedom in full bloom!

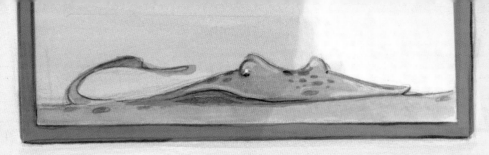

I sneak across the rough wood floor,
    as fast as I can go.
My eight arms latch and then release.

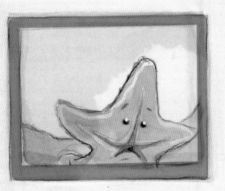

My sense of excitement grows!

But can I leave my life, my friends,
and all I've ever known?
My hearts say...Yes! Today's the day
to strike out on my own.

The sea lies just ahead of me,
so in and down I dive.

I'm falling fast toward what's to come.
I've never felt so alive!

I plunge. I swim. I breathe. I whirl.

I float. I spin. I glide!

I'll follow my heart wherever it leads.
I'll travel far and wide!

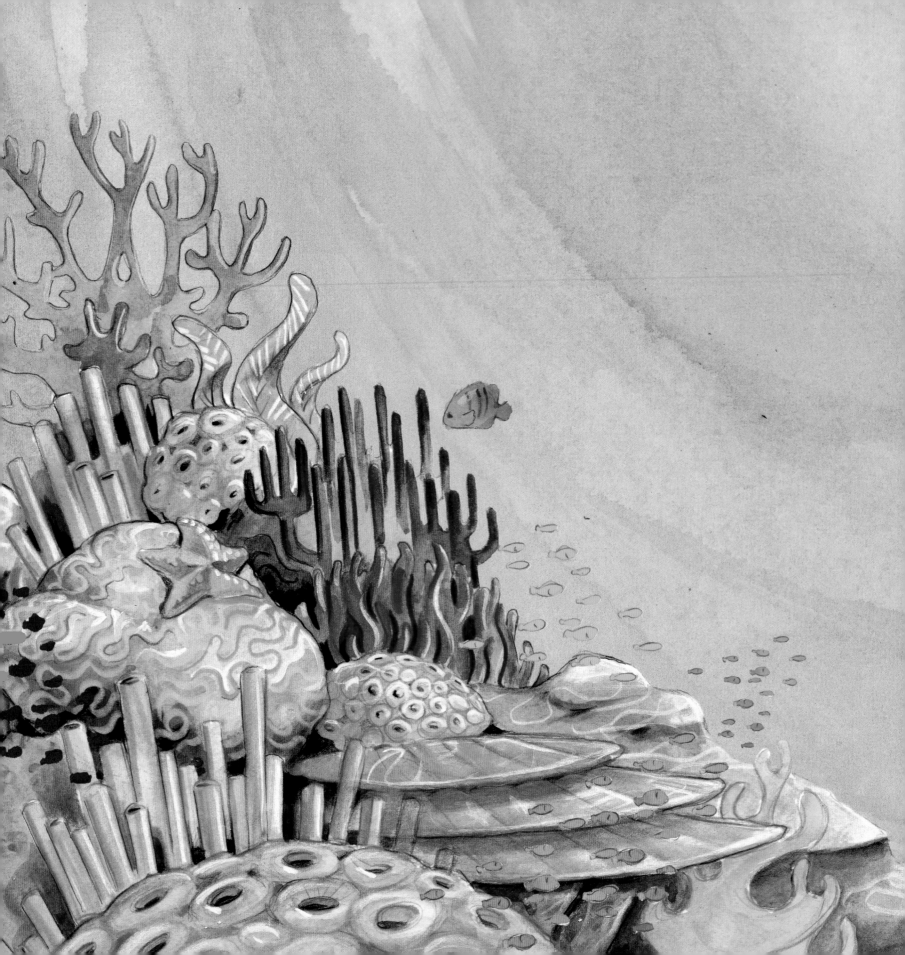

Out of my tank, at last I'm free.
Long may I journey the splendid sea!

INKY'S
INGENIOUS ESCAPE

The **triumphant** true story!

Inky in his tank, before his escape

The book you've just read is based on the real-life story of Inky the octopus, who escaped from the National Aquarium of New Zealand in 2016. After Inky was found injured in a crayfish pot, he was taken to the aquarium for recovery where he lived for two years with a tank mate named Blotchy. One night, the lid of Inky's tank was left slightly open by mistake. Based on arm "prints" found on the floor the next morning, workers at the aquarium believe Inky squeezed through the opening in his tank, slid down the side, and slithered across the floor. Octopuses like Inky are nimble contortionists able to pass through openings as small as a coin! The only explanation for Inky's escape is that, once free of his tank, he squeezed through an even smaller opening—a drain hole only six inches wide—and miraculously made it out to sea.

Inky left his tank mate Blotchy behind in favor of the challenge and allure of the escape. He "didn't even leave us a message," the aquarium manager said. Escape artists and marine biologists alike hope this Houdini of the sea is now happily swimming across the open ocean!

NATIONAL AQUARIUM OF NEW ZEALAND

ABOUT THE AQUARIUM

Inky's former home at the National Aquarium of New Zealand in Napier was the country's first aquarium, with its beginnings stretching back to 1956. Today, this aquarium is home to over one hundred diverse animals from New Zealand and around the world! With a goal of protecting natural habitats and biodiversity, the aquarium works closely with scientists, schools, and the community.

OTHER
ODD
OCTOPUSES

FLO

In 2009, an octopus at the Santa Monica Pier Aquarium in California flooded the aquarium with about two hundred gallons of seawater. The relatively small but very handy octopus, Flo, took apart a water valve in her tank, letting seawater pour out for about ten hours until the first aquarium worker arrived at the scene of the crime!

OTTO

One night at the Sea Star Aquarium in Coburg, Germany, in 2008, all the lights went out. The electricity was fixed in the morning, but it went out again the next night, and the next. So aquarium workers settled in for an all-night stakeout. The culprit: an octopus named Otto. The workers had trained Otto to squirt water at visitors, and Otto figured out that he could put this skill to another use: squirting water at the light above his tank to turn off all the lights! Otto was also known to enjoy playing with a chess board, until he grew bored of it and tossed it away—right out of the aquarium!

SID

Sid the octopus tried escaping the Portobello Aquarium in New Zealand several times before aquarium workers decided to release him back into open waters in 2009. This aquarium is no stranger to sneaky octopuses. Sid's predecessor, named Harry for Harry Houdini, used to sneak out of his tank to eat crayfish from a neighboring tank. Workers originally thought the missing crayfish was a prank perpetrated by biology students, until Harry was caught replacing the lid on the crayfish tank and returning to his own tank.

ARE YOU SQUIDDING ME?!

A Sucker Born Every Minute

How many tentacles do octopuses have again? Trick question: the answer is zero! Octopuses actually have no *tentacles* at all—they have four pairs of arms, which are different from tentacles in terms of how many suckers they have. Suckers are the circular muscles found all along the underside of each arm—tentacles only have suckers at the tips. Unlike octopuses, squids have both tentacles and arms.

Octopuses? Octopi? Octopodes? Pick your favorite—they're all right! In any case, octopuses are loners. They don't usually travel in groups, so—unlike a school of dolphins or a shoal of fish—there is no official word for a bunch of octopuses.

Want an octopus kiss? No, you really don't. All octopuses have venomous saliva. Although *most* octopus venom is not powerful enough to be dangerous to humans, certain species like the tiny blue-ringed octopus could paralyze a person within minutes.

Masters of Disguise

If there isn't time to escape ocean predators such as eels, dolphins, or sharks, an octopus can camouflage itself in less than a second! Octopus skin can blend in with an octopus's surroundings to hide it in plain sight, or can mimic the appearance of a more dangerous animal to scare the predator away. Even if an octopus does get caught and a predator chomps off an arm, the octopus doesn't become a septopus—it can grow back its arms!

Octopuses have beaks! The beak is on the underside of the octopus, where all the arms meet. The octopus uses the beak to break open clam shells, and it has a barbed tongue (called a *radula*) that can scrape out the meat inside. The beak is the only hard part of the octopus's body, and an octopus can contort its body so nimbly that it can fit through nearly any space wide enough to fit its beak.

Octopuses range widely in size. From the top of the head to the tip of the longest arm, the smallest octopus (*Octopus wolfi*) is shorter than one inch long, whereas the biggest octopus (the giant Pacific octopus, *Enteroctopus dofleini*) can grow up to sixteen feet! Scientists discovered one tiny pink octopus that is so cute, they might name it *Opisthoteuthis adorabilis*. (It's true!)

Three hearts and nine brains are better than one! Swimming with eight arms is exhausting! That's why octopuses have three hearts for extra help: two to pump blood to the gills (so they can breathe!) and a third to keep blood moving throughout the rest of the body. An octopus also has one central brain, but two thirds of its neurons are found in its arms rather than its head. That's why some scientists say octopuses' arms have minds of their own! An octopus is able to multitask like a champ, able to open a shellfish with one arm while using another to explore or another to taste food!

Three hundred different species of octopuses have been discovered by scientists! While all octopuses live in salt water, they live in different regions—some live deep down on the cold ocean's floor while others live in warm shallow water.

Octopuses have no bones! Octopuses are invertebrates, which is what scientists call creatures with no backbones. They have no skeleton at all, in fact. This is part of what makes octopuses such great natural escape artists!

Watch out for spilled ink! If an octopus feels threatened, it can release a cloud of blinding black liquid into the water. Just like a superhero's smoke bomb, this cloud of ink temporarily blinds attackers, blocks their sense of smell, and allows this underwater ninja to disappear without a trace.

You Touch It, You Taste It

An octopus's sense of touch is so powerful that the suckers on its arms allow it to taste whatever it is touching! Imagine being able to taste whatever you want before putting it in your mouth. Your parents would never be able to say, "Just try it—you'll like it!" ever again. Octopuses really have it made.

A spiral-shelled mollusk with tentacles called the nautilus is actually a relative of the octopus! *Cephalopods* is the name scientists use for sea animals like the octopus, the squid, and the nautilus, which all share common biological traits such as being exclusively marine animals with large heads and long arms or tentacles.

BIBLIOGRAPHY

Bilefsky, Dan, "Inky the Octopus Escapes From a New Zealand Aquarium," *New York Times*, April 13, 2016, https://www.nytimes.com/2016/04/14/world/asia/inky-octopus-new-zealand-aquarium.html

Bradford, Alina, "Octopus Facts," Live Science, June 8, 2017, https://www.livescience.com/55478-octopus-facts.html

Encyclopaedia Britannica Online, s.v. "octopus," accessed September 1, 2017, https://www.britannica.com/animal/octopus-mollusk

"Legging it: Evasive octopus who has been allowed to look for love," *Independent*, February 14, 2009, http://www.independent.co.uk/environment/nature/legging-it-evasive-octopus-who-has-been-allowed-to-look-for-love-1609168.html

Merriam-Webster Online, s.v. "octopus," accessed September 1, 2017, http://unabridged.merriam-webster.com/unabridged/octopus

"Octopus floods Santa Monica Pier Aquarium," *Los Angeles Times*, February 27, 2009, http://articles.latimes.com/2009/feb/27/local/me-octopus27

"The Story Of An Octopus Named Otto," *All Things Considered*, NPR, November 2, 2008, http://www.npr.org/templates/story/story.php?storyId=96476905

University of Melbourne. "All Octopuses Are Venomous: Could Lead To Drug Discovery." ScienceDaily. https://www.sciencedaily.com/releases/2009/04/090415102215.htm (accessed September 1, 2017).

The full color art was prepared with Liquidtex Soft Body paints and Prismacolor pencils on Arches watercolor paper.

Published by Sourcebooks Jabberwocky, an imprint of Sourcebooks, Inc.
P.O. Box 4410, Naperville, Illinois 60567-4410
(630) 961-3900
Fax: (630) 961-2168
sourcebooks.com

Library of Congress Cataloging-in-Publication Data is on file with the publisher.

Source of Production: Leo Paper, Heshan City, Guangdong Province, China
Date of Production: September 2019
Run Number: 5016364

Printed and bound in China.
LEO 10 9 8 7 6 5 4

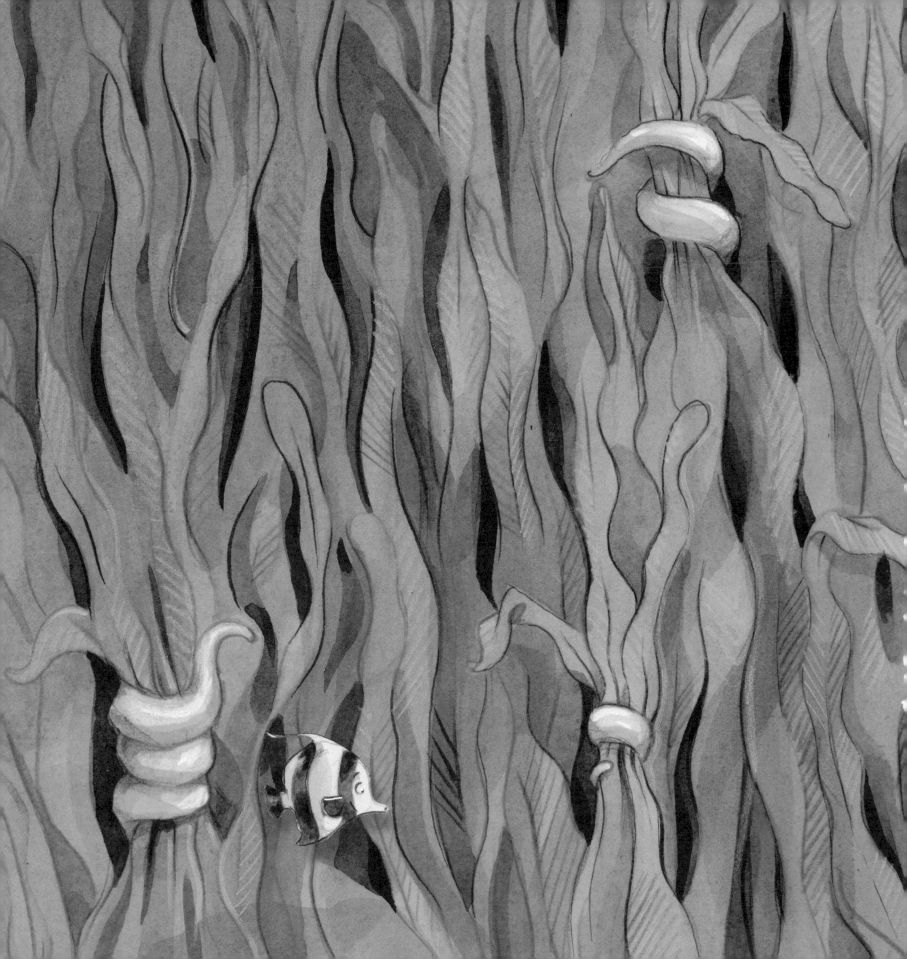